Shadow From The Stone

By Phillip M. Suarez

This work of fiction is registered with the United States Register of Copyrights.

Registration Number: TXu 2-281-290

Effective Date of Registration: September 23, 2021

Registration Decision Date: October 12, 2021

TABLE OF CONTENTS

DEDICATION

This story is dedicated to the man that created the protagonist of this tale. Very few of us would recognize the name, Johnston McCulley. Born on February 2, 1883, in Ottawa, Illinois, he lived to the age of seventy-five, dying in Los Angeles in 1958. Johnston was a police reporter for the <u>Police Gazette</u> before joining the army during WWI.

After the war he began writing for pulp magazines. Most of his early stories were serialized westerns and crime stories. In 1919 his story <u>The Curse of Capistrano</u> was published in the pulp magazine, <u>All Star Weekly</u>. In 1920 it was turned into the silent movie, <u>The Mask of Zorro</u>, staring Douglas Fairbanks. Without a doubt this character became Johnston's most enduring creation.

Johnston is credited with writing over 1,700 stories: serialized stories, novels, short stories, novelettes, and novellas. Additionally, he has a long list of credits for his work on films and television shows. He was a resident of LA for most of his adult life but never married and had no children.

He was a dedicated writer, that stayed at his chosen vocation for his entire life. Most of the characters he created have been long forgotten. Black Star, The Spider, The Crimson Clown, and Thubwa Tham were once popular figures in weekly and monthly publications.

Johnston McCulley is one name among countless others that have chosen to spend their days creating characters and writing stories to take their readers on journeys of adventure, intrigue, romance, and laughter, but have achieved little notoriety or financial success. Yet, they stay at their task, creating stories to entertain readers.

Any writer would be proud to have had the success of Johnston McCulley. Although little known today, he lives on because his most famous character still touches the hearts and minds of many.

ACKNOWLEDGMENTS

This fictional story takes place in New Mexico and Arizona before they became part of the United States. Spain ruled this land for 300 years but in 1820 Mexico gained its independence from the Spanish Empire. Regardless of which country claimed the territory, it was the traditional lands of native tribes who recognized no other claims. In 1848 Mexico ceded these lands to the United States with the Treaty of Guadalupe Hidalgo ending the Mexican American War.

Without the assistance of the staff of the Center of Southwest Research in the Zimmerman Library at the University of New Mexico, the details of travel along the Camino Real be Norte would have been impossible for me to detail. It started with a plea for help from an unknown writer from Ohio and resulted in an invitation to the library and the assistance of a knowledgeable archivist. I thank the staff of the library for their friendly help and welcoming spirit.

I thank two of my lifelong friends, Pat Fitzgerald and Paul Angelo, who agreed to travel parts of New Mexico with me to do research for this story. They made my research of the area into a fun filled adventure that will forever be a pleasant memory.

As always, I thank my editor, Claire Lober for her efforts and insights and Kirk Poffenberger of Design Studios for his creative design of the cover and his ever-present encouragement. Finally, I have a loyal set of beta-readers who's comments and critiques are invaluable to my efforts to create a readable story. Thank you: Russ Holley, Alec Pendleton, David Waters, Julie Mitchell, and Denny Mitchell.

1.

CHAPTER

1828

The journey had been long and hard for the elegant old man and his servants. Their long journey had started three months prior in Guadalajara. They met their guide, Dominic, and his assistant, Juanito, in Chihuahua before continuing their trek north. The elderly man had become disgusted with the rampant corruption and greed within the Mexican government, which far exceeded that of the former Spanish governors. Although approaching sixty years of age, the elderly gentleman felt that he needed to restart what remained of his life in a new place that would provide fresh opportunities. A new adventure might remove the disappointment of his short time in Mexico City after reluctantly agreeing to represent southern California in the new country's congress. Fortunately, the government of the newly independent Mexico opened trading with the Americans, making Santa Fe a much more important trading center.

The small party traveled to El Paso del Norte following the Camino Real. The large wagon was constructed in the small village of Tonala, just outside of Guadalajara, to the master's specifications. Four large mature oxen pulled the dray through the Chihuahuan desert with little trouble, Dominic carefully avoiding the areas of large sand dunes.

Manolo was the youngest man on the trip and had been his master's valet for six years. He got the position when his great uncle, Bernardo, got too ill to manage the daily duties. His beloved uncle died three years ago, and Manolo still spoke to him every night before saying his prayers. Manolo was surprised by the moves to Mexico City, to Guadalajara, and now to this city in the middle of nowhere, but knew that his obligation was to remain at his master's side.

Safwan was a tall, dark-skinned man who had walked beside the wagon all the way from Guadalajara. Ten years ago, the elderly man was in Cadiz when he saved the Moor from being imprisoned for vagrancy. He most likely would have been sent to Africa and sold into slavery.

The Captain of the Guards conveniently agreed that the Moor was in the employ of the gentleman from California and was just waiting for his master before their trip to America. Their master purchased Safwan's freedom for two gold escudos. The captain could have sold the Moor at the dock for much more, but he didn't have to share these two coins.

The traveling party spent five days in El Paso del Norte, as Dominic attempted to find willing traveling companions into the dangerous Nueva Mexico territory. Manolo's master sat at a shaded table on the veranda of the hotel, sipping a drink, when four men slowly rode down the main street, trying not to kick up dust. Two of them dismounted in front of the hotel, grabbed their saddlebags and rifles. "Find a stable that can manage all the horses, and Custis and I will get us some rooms," the burly bearded leader told the two remaining mounted men. He started to walk toward the steps of the hotel, when he turned back to his men and laughingly called out, "Remember, everyone, takes a bath today."

As the two men walked to the door of the hotel, the leader nodded a greeting toward Manolo's master. The elegant man smiled in return and acknowledged the rugged-looking stocky American with a nod of his own. Fifteen minutes later, the American came out of the hotel and walked to the master's table. "*Buenos tardes, senor,*" he said in greeting.

"Good afternoon," answered the older man. Motioning to the empty chair across from him, he added, "please, join me."

The other man sat and waived to a waiter who had followed him out the door. "I'll have a beer if it's cold, and please give this gentleman another drink," he said.

"Si, senor," the waiter quickly turned and walked back into the hotel.

The master said to the American, "*Muchas gracias,* sir, but that was not necessary. However, I will enjoy the drink and your company."

"Thank you. My name is Thaddeus Clay. I'm leading a ragged bunch of traders on an excursion. There are seven wagons and twelve more men about two days behind us. We had never seen Mexico but have heard much about Chihuahua, so we took some goods down there and are bringing Mexican goods back north."

The Mexican raised his eyebrows, "Sixteen armed Americans' must have alarmed many of the officials that you ran into on your journey."

"Oh, we aren't all Americans," laughed Clay, 'but I had a letter of introduction from the Governor in Santa Fe, which eased the concerns of all we met on our journey through your country." He watched as the waiter placed the drinks on the table and took two backward steps, waiting to see if the American was satisfied with his beer. He took a long sip and smiled at the waiter, "That beer is ice cold. *Muy bueno!*" After the beaming server walked away, Clay turned his attention back to the older Mexican. "We're on our way back from Chihuahua, *senor*. We have enjoyed our trip; many parts of the territory are beautiful, even the desert. If we get back safely, we will have had a very profitable trip."

"Mr. Clay, are you and your men returning directly to Santa Fe?" asked the older man.

"Yes, the men are very anxious to get home." Clay noticed the smile that creased the older man's face. "*Perdoneme,* senor. But may I ask your name?"

"Forgive me, my friend. I am Alonso Quijano from Guadalajara." The noble gentleman silently asked Jesus for forgiveness for his little deceit and promised to correct it at the earliest opportunity. He doubted that the American would recognize the formal name of Cervantes' famous Don Quixote. "I am trying to get to Santa Fe with my four men." The Mexican grinned and took a sip of his drink. "Do you think that we could travel with you and your troop to Santa Fe? We have one large wagon, our own provisions, and spare horses."

"I am sorry to ask, but who are these men that you are traveling with?" asked Mr. Clay.

"Two are household members that have worked for me for many years, and the other two are the guides that I hired to take us to Santa Fe," responded the Mexican gentleman. "The guides are attempting to find a larger group that we can join to make the trip safer. I am beginning to believe that the lead guide has never been north of this dusty little city, although he assured me otherwise."

The hotel manager came onto the veranda and told the American that the baths were ready for him and his men. Thaddeus Clay excused himself and asked his new friend to join him in the dining room after he bathed.

2.

CHAPTER

On the Trail

The trail kept them just to the west of the Rio Grande and east of what seemed to the elderly Mexican as a vast endless desert. The terrain was rough and dusty, but there was more vegetation here than they had seen in months. The growth was mostly sparse-looking trees along waterless riverbanks with occasional patches of wildflowers and weedy bushes. They had traveled almost 475 kilometers over eighteen days when they arrived at Bernalillo, a long-established stop along the old Spanish trail. As the eight wagons entered the small village, the traders were warmly welcomed by the villagers.

Don Diego had advised Mr. Clay of his real name as soon as the wagons got north of Las Cruces. He explained to the American that he didn't want certain members of the Mexican government to know about his intent to relocate to Santa Fe until he was already there.

Manolo drove the wagon, which was pulled by four mules, but Dominic, the supposed guide, asked to be dismissed from his obligation to Don Diego and did not accompany them into Nueva Mexico. Clay's young interpreter insisted that mules were much more suited for the trip than the big oxen. The interpreter was a small young man, no more than five feet, four inches tall, with a countenance well beyond his twenty years. His name was Christopher Carson, but his companions called him "Kit". He spoke excellent Spanish, adequate French, and several Indian languages. He could also communicate with the natives in sign language when necessary.

As the travelers began to tend to the animals. Mr. Clay and Don Diego joined Kit, who was having an animated discussion in Tiwa with an Indian. Kit appeared concerned, asking many questions. Thaddeus and Diego stood silently, anxiously awaiting to hear what the discussion was about.

Kit finally turned to the two men and explained in English, "The Comanche have raided Santa Fe and some of the pueblos in the area. They have stolen many horses, killed a few people, and taken some young people, including the daughter of the Fuentes family in Santa Fe." The young man looked to the north, "The girl's father led some men to rescue his daughter, but he and three others were killed when they accidentally rode into a large group of Comanche raiders."

"What of the girl?" asked Don Diego.

"There is no news. She is supposed to be very beautiful, and is only fifteen years old." The young man looked down to the ground, shaking his head, "It's likely she'll become some brave's wife, accepted by the men and hated by the women, especially if she is not the first wife of the brave."

"And the others?"

"Two young Indian servants, a boy, and a girl, were taken from the same family. If they are young enough, the tribe will adopt them, and quickly give them to a family who has lost someone recently." He glanced at the Mexican, "It's good for the tribe; it gets new blood into the tribe." He seemed unfazed as he continued, "It's the way it works around here, *senor*. The tribes steal young captives from each other, including the Spanish." He waited to see how Don Diego would respond.

The Mexican asked another question, "Who is the fourth person?"

"The young girl's maid," Kit looked at Don Diego and asked, "Her *doncella*?"

"Yes, I understand, an older woman who assists the daughter and is her companion until she reaches maturity or marries." Diego asked yet another question, "What will happen to the *doncella*?"

"Unless she herself is a beauty and catches the attention of a warrior, she will be raped and killed before the war party returns to their people," the young interpreter said bluntly. He then turned and walked toward the wagons.

"Where are you going?" shouted Diego.

"I'm going to get the children. That Pueblo," indicating the Indian that told him about the Comanche, "tracked the raiders. They split into two groups; the larger group will continue to raid, and the other contains the hostages and the stolen horses. They hid the hostages and the horses in a closed canyon with only three guards watching them. If we can get there before the raiding party returns, we may be able to rescue them."

Don Diego followed the young man back to the wagons. "Safwan and I are going with you," he announced.

"It will be a hard ride, and you have to be willing to kill," Kit said, challenging the older man.

Diego nodded, "Don't worry about us keeping up. I've had to kill before. We will follow your orders."

"At dawn, we're leaving with or without you," Clay advised them. "We'll stay on the main trail, Kit. We'll get as far as we can tomorrow and hope to make La Cienega the following day. We'll rest for only one night there. We'll keep moving along as quickly as we can. The news of the Comanche raids has made everyone anxious to get home."

Diego took Manolo aside and told him quietly that he and Juanito were to stay with the wagon and follow the others. They were to complete the journey to Santa Fe, and he was to make sure that Mr. Clay got home safely. Don Diego told the uncertain servant that if Safwan and Diego did not join him within a month, everything in the wagon was his to do with as he chose. He added that Manolo should give Juanito enough to start a good life in Santa Fe. He closed by telling his servant that he trusted his judgment and knew that he would do what was best.

Manolo bowed slightly and said, "As you wish, Don Diego."

3.

CHAPTER

The Rescue

Within fifteen minutes, the four men headed out, each riding a saddled mule. Safwan led a tan-colored mare behind him, and Diego led his black stallion. Their goal was a closed canyon on the north end of the Sandia Mountains. Three hours later, they stopped for the night, only a half mile from their goal. Kit and the Tiwa decided that they would make their assault at first light.

The Comanche guards had set up their camp in an area that had much more vegetation than what Diego had anticipated. The Tiwa told them that the two groups had split at the Rio Grande. The raiders went west, likely to strike some pueblos in search of additional horses and hostages. However, they would not go too far because they would be careful to avoid the Navajo. Also, the stolen horses would need water in a day or so.

In the pre-dawn, Kit gave simple instructions, and once everyone was in place, he immediately charged the encampment. They killed two Comanche and ran off the third. The four hostages were frightened but in good health. With regret, the rescuers had to scatter the stolen horses and started their return journey to the Camino Real.

Kit was pleasantly surprised that Diego and Safwan held up to the physical demands of the past twelve hours. He expected that Diego would not hesitate to attack the captors but was astounded by how well and confidently the old gentlemen moved during the attack. He ran quickly, with a grace that belied his graying hair. Safwan moved without hesitation, and had a remarkably quiet and quick step, allowing Kit to get into place without detection, and his one shot was true. He killed the Indian closest to the hostages as Kit ran toward them from Safwan's far right. Kit thought if Safwan missed, the Indian would look in the direction of the shot, giving Kit an opportunity to get a clear shot. The second shot was not needed.

Teresa, the Spanish girl, rode the tan horse. The *doncella*, whose name was Gabriella, convinced

Diego that she could handle his big black stallion. The young Navajo boy rode behind Diego, and the Pueblo girl rode with Kit. Carson led the group west-northwest back toward the Camino Real, hoping to find an adequate place to wait for the wagon train to arrive.

"We have only four men and limited weapons. If we don't meet up with the wagon train quickly, we will need cover and shelter for us and our animals. When the Comanche learn of their two dead braves, they will come for us," Carson said this while keeping his eyes on the horizon to his west and north. "They need those horses, so they will first try to recover as many of those that they can. Right now, the young brave that got away is trying to corral as many of them as he can."

They rode through the open country under the hot September sun for many hours until they came upon a small outcropping of rock that stood no higher than the height of two men. Kit stayed with the group as the Pueblo, whose Spanish name was Saturnino, rode ahead a short way to see if he could see signs of the wagon train.

When Saturnino returned and told Kit that the wagon train had already passed this area, Kit told everyone that they would spend the night where they were and head out before the first light. Don Diego and Saturnino took the first watch, the Pueblo taking a high spot on the outcropping and Diego taking a spot about a hundred yards to the west. Diego sat on the hard ground with a blanket over his shoulders, watching the western horizon for any sign of trouble. It was a clear night, the temperature falling to a cold chill with countless stars shining brightly above.

After a half hour or so, Diego heard soft footsteps approaching him from behind. He turned and was surprised to find Gabriella walking towards him.

"Excuse me, Patron, but I could not sleep. Do you mind if I sit with you for a while?"

"You're welcome to join me, but you must speak very softly," replied Diego. "Please do not call me Patron. I am simply Diego." He hesitated as he saw that his words confused her. "Senorita, if you must, you can address me as Don Diego, but I prefer that you use my given name," he added with a broad smile.

Gabriella spoke softly, "This land has so much beauty and yet is harsh and frightening."

Diego looked straight ahead into the western night, "Kit tells me that out there is the land of the Navajo. He says they are fierce fighters but seldom leave their own lands."

"So, how different are they than the Comanche?"

"The Navajo tend to stay on their own lands. The Comanche, go wherever they wish and are great horsemen."

The *doncella* was just short of thirty years old, but had the figure and appearance of a much younger woman. She had reddish brown hair, which she now had tied back, displaying her high cheekbones and clear skin. "Are you from Nueva Mexico, Don Diego?" she asked, clearly testing the sound of addressing him so informally.

"No, Gabriella. I was born in California, which is where I lived all my life except for the last four years." He added, "This is my first trip to Nueva Mexico."

"Why would you leave California for this dry, harsh land?"

"Actually I left Jalisco to come here. I left California four years ago and have been looking for a new home since. I have been told that Santa Fe is a place of opportunity, a good place to start over." He moved his gaze from the horizon to the intriguing woman sitting next to him. "Are you a native of Santa Fe?"

"No, I was born in San Luis Potisi," she smiled as she thought of that beautiful town. "My father arranged a marriage for me with the son of a wealthy landowner from Santa Fe. I was sent to my betrothed when I was sixteen years of age. I turned seventeen on the journey to Santa Fe. When I arrived, I learned that Domingo had died two months prior from some strange sickness he caught on a trek to explore an ancient pueblo named Pecos. They buried him near a crossing of a river not far from the pueblo and named the crossing 'Gabriella'. They told me that he held a letter from me in his hand throughout his last day."

"Could you have returned to your home?' asked the curious Diego.

"I suppose I could have," Gabriella looked up at the stars, "but it would have been difficult to do so. It would have cost me my entire dowry, and the return journey would have been dangerous. My cousin had married into a family in Santa Fe and was the one that recommended me as a prospective bride to Domingo's father. When I arrived, Lupe and Raphael allowed me to live with them, eventually asking me to become the *doncella* to their daughter. Teresa was only three years old at the time and was a lovely child. I have been with her ever since."

"Is Raphael, *senor* Fuentes?" asked Diego.

"Yes, that is his name."

Diego hesitated, and looked at the beautiful, sad woman. "I'm afraid there is bad news that I must tell you, *senorita*." He looked into the eyes of the younger woman, "*Senor* Fuentes and three others were killed by a band of Indians as they tried to track the raiding party to rescue you and Teresa."

Gabriella's wide eyes showed the shock of this news, but she remained silent. She then placed her head on Diego's shoulder and began to weep. He softly put an arm around her and tenderly held her, keeping his eyes on the dark horizon. They stayed in that platonic embrace for more than ten minutes. The only movements were a gentle rocking back and forth by Diego and Gabriella, occasionally dabbing her eyes with the sleeve of her garment.

Gabriella broke the silence, "We must not say a word about this to Teresa until we are safe. The heartbreak of her father's death, in her already fragile condition, would cause too much grief for her to handle." Obviously embarrassed, she took her head off his shoulder and moved slightly away. "Pardon me, Don Diego. I didn't mean to be so forward."

He quickly responded, "No pardon is necessary, Gabriella. The news required comforting. Besides, holding a beautiful woman under this magnificent night sky, was a pleasure."

"Your wife might not think so, Don Diego."

"Unfortunately, my wife died many years ago," he replied. Gabriella sat quietly, allowing him time to decide if he would say more. "She and our baby son died during childbirth."

"I'm so sorry," she commented as she laid her left hand on his right arm.

"Thank you, but it was long ago." Diego then explained how excited they were in anticipation of their first child. The hacienda had been prepared for the arrival of the new family member, the servants were joyous with thoughts of a baby to care for, and even the *vaqueros* demonstrated a high degree of expectation. The loss of his wife and newborn son devastated Diego, causing him to go into a deep depression. For a year, he did nothing but wallow in his grief, ignoring his responsibilities and drinking too much wine. Then one day, he went to see his favorite horse, Toronado, who he hadn't seen in months. The big black horse not only would not come to him but ran from him if Diego tried to get close. When a teary-eyed Diego complained to his valet that even his horse had deserted him, Bernardo slapped him across the face and told him that the horse, like all of those that loved him, did not know this man that he had become. The slap from this mute man startled Diego but drove him to regain the respect of this man that he loved.

They both were surprised that three hours had gone by so quickly when they heard Safwan approaching to relieve Diego. "*Patron*, you better get some sleep," Safwan said to Don Diego. He hid his surprise at seeing Gabriella but told her, "I checked on the girl. She is still sleeping."

Gabriella looked embarrassed, wondering if Safwan was scolding her for abandoning Teresa's side. "Pardon me,' she said to both men, 'I must go to Teresa."

Diego walked with her back to the campsite and said softly, "He meant no disrespect. I think he just wanted you to know that he will help you keep the girl safe."

4.

CHAPTER

Rejoining the Caravan

Carson had them mounted and ready to leave just before sunrise. There was a *paraje*, a watering stop, where the horses could drink their fill and eat some grass not far up the trail. He hoped that Mr. Clay had stopped there for the night. After a few hours at a moderate pace, they arrived at the *paraje*. The mules and horses became excited as they smelled the water and grasslands. Kit made the riders stop and wait a short distance from their target as Saturnino rode ahead to see if it was safe to ride into the area. The Pueblo saw no evidence of hostiles in the area but did find a note under three stacked rocks indicating that the wagon train would stop at Tamaya Pueblo and then move on to Kewa Pueblo. The travelers spent a quiet night at the old rest area, the men standing guard in pairs as they had done the night before, and as she had done the night before, Gabriella sat with Don Diego through his watch.

Although the trail was not that difficult, the increase in altitude affected the humans and the mules, so the going was slow, causing the travelers to be even more anxious as they watched for the raiding Comanche. They were exhausted and extremely hungry when they approached the Tamaya village. Kit and the Saturnino learned that they were only a few hours behind Mr. Clay.

They rested for a few hours as Kit bartered with the locals for fresh mules. The man with whom he bartered refused any deal that did not include Diego's black stallion. Although the tribe was primarily an agrarian culture, the members were proud horsemen, and this man knew that he would likely never see a horse like Oscuro again. Diego settled the issue by offering the tribesman two gold Spanish doubloons, a currency still accepted throughout the Americas. The Tamayan countered by asking for four, raising four fingers as he smiled at Don Diego. The elderly Diego refused to budge from his original offer, crossing his arms and raising his chin, indicating that he felt to respond to the Tamayan's counteroffer was beneath his dignity. To which the Tamayan took on a similar stance and attitude.

After many minutes, with neither man changing his stance or position, Diego motioned for the negotiator to follow him. He walked beyond the wall of a small adobe structure with the Tamaya at his side. Don Diego made sure no one could see the two men before he turned his attention to the negotiator. He raised two fingers of his left hand, pointed toward the mules with the index finger of his right hand, and made a circular motion. He then raised the index finger of his left hand and pointed at the Tamaya with his right index finger, followed that by covering his own mouth with his left hand, and shaking his head back and forth slowly. The Tamaya smiled and nodded in acceptance. Diego gave him one doubloon, which he put into a pouch he carried at his waist. The two men then returned to the waiting group.

As they walked back to Carson and the others, the negotiator waived his left arm angrily and told the group in a voice full of disgust that he agreed to the Mexican's terms. Don Diego nodded to Kit and then handed two doubloons to the Tamayan negotiator.

With the fresh animals, the rescue party was able to catch up to the wagon train before it reached the Kewa Pueblo.

5.

CHAPTER

Kewa Pueblo

The main wagon train was within an hour or so of reaching the Kewa Pueblo, when the rescuers and hostages caught up to it. None was more excited to see their return than Manolo, who dismounted from his horse and ran to greet Don Diego. He talked excitedly as he walked next to his master, holding the bridle of the big black horse.

Most of the natives of the pueblo came to the main courtyard staring at the travelers and showing great curiosity about the items within the carts. Carson and Saturnino were greeted warmly by an elderly man who appeared to be the spokesman for the pueblo. After hearing about the rescue of the hostages, the spokesman's wife came and led the four former hostages into the pueblo. Don Diego showed concern as the group disappeared around the corner of a structure but was assured by Kit that the women would care for the hostages. They would bathe and feed them while checking to see if they had any injuries that needed attending.

"Every pueblo and village in this area has suffered the loss of loved ones through kidnapping by raiders. We all celebrate the rescue and return of a hostage as if it is one of our own," Kit explained to Don Diego. He added with a knowing smile, "Don't worry, the doncella will be fine."

Diego blushed slightly but added, "What of the Navajo boy? I am certain the people of this pueblo have been raided by the Navajo."

"The Navajo have been their biggest fear for as long as they have lived,' answered Carson, 'but they know that the boy has been taken twice from his home. First, he was taken from his Navajo family by the Spanish and now has been stolen from his Spanish family by the Comanche. They know what the boy has gone through."

After washing off the dirt and dust from the trail and being fed, the four rescuers and Mr. Clay sat in a clean, cool adobe home with the pueblo leaders. The natives were anxious to hear of the

Comanche raid and the rescue of the hostages. They sat quietly as Saturnino told the story of the hostile raid and subsequent rescue, carefully detailing the part that each rescuer played. The tribesmen nodded in satisfaction at the end of the tale. One of the Pueblo pointed his chin toward Safwan and spoke for a few minutes to both Saturnino and Carson. Carson explained to Diego that the Indians were curious about Safwan. They had never seen a man with skin as dark as his and asked if he had been burnt. Since Safwan had not spoken since they arrived in the pueblo, they wondered if he could speak and, most importantly, wanted to know where he came from.

Don Diego asked Saturnino if any of the men spoke Spanish. He responded by saying that all of them spoke Spanish, but he and Kit spoke to them in their native tongue as a sign of respect and gratitude. He then turned to the Kewa elders and spoke to them in Spanish.

"Forgive me for speaking in my native tongue, for I am new to this land. I am Diego Vega and," indicating the Moor, "my companion is called Safwan, which means rock or pure." Diego then asked Safwan to tell them about himself.

The Kewas were amazed at the deep, resonant tone of his voice as he explained where he came from and how Don Diego had saved him from slavery. They were startled to hear that there were a great many men and women that looked like him and many with even darker skin color. They nodded in approval when he mentioned his commitment to his God. They didn't know of the God he spoke of but understood that Safwan called Him, Allah.

The men were interrupted when the head elder's wife entered the dwelling with the four captives, who were dressed in clean Kewa clothing. The Navajo boy wore simple pants and a tunic made of rough cloth. The two younger women wore dresses of the same material with colorful sashes at their waists. Their hair had been washed, brushed, and tied back into two long tails. Gabriella was dressed much differently. Her dress was made of animal hide and had a colorful stitching design on her chest and back. Her hair was tied back into a single tail, and a blue cloth ribbon was tied above each ear. Diego stared at her, wondering if everyone could hear his heart beating because the hard, fast beat was exploding in his ears.

Kit leaned into Diego and whispered into his ear, "The dress of animal hide is a symbol of great respect for her. The making of that dress took many months and much effort."

Diego smiled in appreciation but asked, "Why did they do so?"

"Saturnino told them about her courage trying to protect Teresa from the Comanche."

The wagon train spent the next two days at the pueblo, resting the animals and preparing for the final part of the long journey, hoping that they would avoid the Comanche raiders. Diego and Gabriella spent much of those two days in each other's company, walking about the pueblo, sharing stories from their lives, speaking to the men of the wagon train, and enjoying the kindness of the pueblo families. One afternoon they rode out to some nearby ancient pueblos that had been abandoned for over a hundred years after the Pueblo Rebellion of 1680. It was in the quiet walled ruins they shared their first intimate moment of passion. As they rode slowly back to the main pueblo, Diego professed his love to Gabriella and asked that she become his wife, worried that the difference in age would discourage the much younger woman. Her response was that she had felt bound to Diego since the first moment she looked into his eyes.

When the traders left the Kiwa pueblo, Thaddeus Clay placed Diego's wagon in the middle of the caravan. Diego and Gabriella rode next to the wagon with the children in front of them. Safwan usually rode on the other side of the wagon but would assist the other travelers when needed. Since the Moor was much younger and stronger than Diego, it was agreed that he would give assistance wherever he was needed. Even if he was at the front or rear of the wagon train, he always kept a careful watch on his master and the children.

6.

CHAPTER

Making a Stand

On the second day after leaving the Kiwa Pueblo, the wagon train came to an area of wetlands known as La Cienega. Carson kept the travelers on high alert, assuring that the wagons and animals were kept close by, watering the animals in stages, and assigning guards to always be near the animals.

Mr. Clay approached Carson with Diego at his side. "Kit, we're being extremely cautious, considering we haven't seen any hostiles. Certainly, that raiding party would be making their way home by now."

The young man waited before answering his boss, "They're watching us and will let us git to a place where they plan to attack us. It will be a place where they will have the betters of us. We have more guns than them, more men than them, and they need to do more than hit and run."

"Why is that, *compadre*?" asked Diego.

"Well, their raiding started out good, but then they lost all their hostages and all the horses they stole. On top of that, they lost the two young braves that we killed." Kit looked to the west, "After they left the three men to watch the horses they stole, the raiding party went west. Who knows how successful they had been? If they had run into a large group of Navajo, they would have had to fight their way out of trouble. They could be crazy angry at this point and need to spill some blood and get back their hostages."

Clay became very agitated during this discussion. "What in all blazes are we going to do about this? Just continue up the trail until they attack?"

"No, sir. We'll stay on the trail for another three miles or so and then head east as quickly as we can. There is an old, abandoned pueblo to the east where we can make a stand."

The following evening the travelers and their animals were entrenched within the walls of the forsaken pueblo. Fortunately, among the collapsing abandoned structures were two large buildings that were arranged adjacent to one another, separated by only twenty feet. Carson placed wagons wall to wall in the open space between the two structures, which created a small courtyard and allowed for relatively safe movement between them. Of course, guarding their trade goods was critically important to the traders, so men were positioned near the wagons to protect them from the Comanche.

Diego marveled at the old structures. The roofs had fallen long ago, and the wood from those would have been removed and reused for various purposes. The stone walls were amazingly straight, with sharp right angles in the corners. The doorways were also perfectly squared with large wooden lintels supporting the stone above. It appeared that the people who built these structures must have been shorter than modern men because only the youngest of the travelers could walk through a doorway without bending down considerably. After three or four centuries, many of the stone walls still stood, providing some protection for those fortunate enough to find them.

The experienced drovers and Carson knew that the most likely danger at night was the theft of horses and property or a silent assault on a sleeping guard. It was during daylight that the Comanche would mount a full attack. They are not a people to make a prolonged siege. Their style of fighting was a quick raid with limited loss of life. Kit thought the most likely action would be a fast attack by a limited number of braves to test the strength of the defenders and to seek out any weak spots. The warriors would retreat only to be followed by a larger, more aggressive assault. If the traders were able to kill or wound a good number of the Comanche in the two attacks, it is most likely that they would leave. This raiding party had been on the move for some time and would need to return to their people, even if empty-handed.

That night the Comanche tried to determine if there were any weak spots in the perimeter of the travelers' shelter. The anxious defenders fired a few errant shots into the dark night without hitting anything but New Mexico. The sound of the musket fire kept the group of anxious travelers awake and on edge. The Indians slipped back into the darkness. They waited until their quarry once again became comfortable in the dark night. Then they began to shoot fire-lit arrows into the travelers' compound. They continued to shoot a few arrows every ten or fifteen minutes, forcing the weary voyagers into a sleepless night.

Just before dawn, the Comanche made their first attack. Although they never came close to breaching the perimeter, they did manage to kill one *camionero* and seriously wound a second. The attacking war party appeared to have about fifteen warriors, which was more than Carson had anticipated. The second attack came shortly after the first and was concentrated on the eastern barricade. Although this attack was briefer than the first, it was costlier for both sides. A single Comanche was able to get to the small window in the stone ruin and killed two mules with two lightning-fast shots from his bow. He was driven away by an infuriated *camionero* and shot by Carson as he tried to flee. Another brave was wounded and carried to safety by two others. One of Clay's men took an arrow in his left shoulder, but fortunately, no major vessels were hit. The concern was whether the tip had been treated with poison or not.

"They're done for today," announced Carson.

"How can you be sure?" Diego quickly asked.

"They will mourn their dead and rest. The tribe cannot afford to lose young men. There ain't enough of them."

"Will they come again tonight?"

"No, sir," Kit declared. "I figure they'll fire their flaming arrows again, but this time they will concentrate on trying to hit the animals. We lose a few more mules, and we'll have to consider leaving a wagon or two behind. Hell, we'll be slowed down considerably at best."

Diego went to check on Gabriella and Teresa and found Manolo and Safwan hovering near them and the other two rescued hostages. Diego could no longer hide his affection for Gabriella. They embraced tenderly without any concern for what the others thought.

"Kit says they will not attack today," he explained. "However, they will do their best to prevent us from sleeping tonight."

"They will continue to shoot fire at us?" Gabriella asked.

"Yes," replied Diego as he nodded. He looked at his servants, saying, "Let's make sure everyone gets some sleep during the daylight in case we are kept busy tonight.

"Yes, *Patron*," they both replied.

"Manolo, come with me to check on Oscuro and the other animals."

The two men were greeted by a whinny from the big stallion.

"He is restless," suggested Manolo.

"He doesn't like missing the action," explained the older man. "He knows that he is a defenseless target in these ruins." He patted Manolo on the shoulder and added, "However, I think tonight he will get to do what he was intended to do." He then explained to Manolo what he wanted him to do.

7.

CHAPTER

The Rider in Black Returns

As soon as the New Mexico sky began to darken, Diego held Gabriella close to him and then looked deeply into her eyes, "I love you, *mi belleza*. Try to rest. I must go and see how I can help Kit."

She gently touched his handsome face with her right hand and looked longingly into his eyes. Sensing that there was something troubling him, she pleaded, "Stay with me, Diego. They won't need you until daylight."

He smiled and lied, "I will be back before you realize that I am gone." With that, he left her in Safwan's care and went to join Manolo.

He found his servant waiting for him as they had discussed. Manolo had retrieved Diego's black clothing: boots, shirt, pants, hat, and mask from the secret compartment built under the bed of their wagon. Oscuro was saddled and anxious to run. The trusted servant quickly helped his master put on his riding boots, carefully tied the mask to Diego's head, and fastened his rapier around his waist.

"Manolo, a third of what I have goes to Gabriella, a third goes to you, and the last third goes to Safwan. Make sure our young muleskinner gets enough to start a new life in Santa Fe." Diego looked into his servant's eyes with tenderness and paternal pride. "I trust you with all I own and all I love."

"Patron, I am sure that you will see us soon. Certainly, God will protect you, as He has always done."

Don Diego Vega patted his friend and servant on his shoulders with both hands and simply said, "Perhaps."

With that, the man once known as Zorro, mounted his black stallion and waved to his tearful companion. Oscuro easily cleared the gap between two wagons, and the horse and rider rode into the night.

"What's he doing?" Mr. Clay demanded of Manolo. "The old scoundrel isn't running, is he?"

Manolo was aflame with anger to hear this man insult his master. He was just about to attack the leader of the wagon train when he felt a strong hand garb his shoulder. He turned to find Kit Carson shaking his head.

"He isn't runnin', Mr. Clay. I suspect that he is going to try to distract the Comanche to give us time to make a run for it." Carson looked at Manolo and added, "It's not in his nature to run. I don't know why that old man thinks he can do it or how he's planning to do it, but we better be prepared to move quickly if he does it."

Manolo smiled at Carson and nodded. "That is true, *Senor* Carson. He has done such things before, but that was many years ago. But his horse is young and fast, and his will is stronger than ever. He can be as quiet as a calm wind and as crafty as a fox."

"I'm sorry for what I said, Manolo," said Clay. "I was speaking without thinking. I believe that Senor Vega is an honorable and courageous man. I was just so surprised to see him riding out. Why didn't he speak to us about his plan?"

Manolo stared straight into the larger man's eyes, "Because you would have tried to stop him."

Clay snorted and then added, "You're right. We would have."

Once Diego was a short distance from the ruins, he slowed Oscuro to a steady walk. "Be patient, my friend," he whispered to the black stallion. "Shortly, we will have to run fast and long." Diego strained his eyes to see in the dark desert. He knew from what direction the Comanche approached the ruins, so he assumed their camp was to the west-northwest. After a short while, he thought he saw dust rising in the night sky, indicating the movement of horse and man. He assumed a few of the braves were moving forward to get within arrow range of the ancient pueblo in which his friends and loved ones waited.

He turned Oscuro slightly to his right, hoping to find the Comanche camp before he was noticed by any of the raiders. When he thought he saw the light of a small fire, he got down from his horse. He told Oscuro to wait for his call and quickly walked toward the rear of what he hoped was the camp. After five minutes, he saw what he was looking for, the string of stolen horses. He slowly approached the horses with caution. He knew that a whinny or a snort from a single horse could give his presence away to the nearby braves. Diego softly hummed a Spanish melody, hoping that it would calm the excitable mustangs. He stood straight and continued to hum as he walked toward a large stallion. The beast's alert eyes opened wide, and his ears stood erect as they listened to the dark approaching man.

Diego gently grabbed the rope that ran around the horse's neck, which was tied to another rope that was strung from two bushes. He determined that half of the small herd were similarly attached to the same rope. Diego slowly removed a knife from his belt and quickly cut the rope that bound the horses to the bushes. The horses stirred but clearly did not fear this man. He then cautiously walked to the horses secured to a rope that ran to another scraggily bush.

Diego moved slowly amongst the small herd and then moved toward where he hoped Oscuro waited. After a hundred feet, he whistled softly. He continued forward and turned his head to look behind him. To his relief, he saw no sign that he had been discovered. To his surprise, he saw a few of the mustangs following him.

Oscuro walked up to his master calmly and quietly. Diego hoisted himself up into his saddle and began to ride toward the west. After a short while, he nudged Oscuro, and they started to canter away from the Comanche camp. When Diego heard loud voices from the camp, he kicked his heels into the stallion's flanks, causing the powerful beast to gallop through the desert night. Diego glanced behind him to see mustangs galloping after them. Although he couldn't see if some of the Comanche were following, he assumed that they were and continued his fast pace to the west until he saw the outline of trees. He slowed as he approached what he assumed was the Rio Grande, halting near the bank of what he feared to be a broad river. Instead he found that the broad riverbed contained only a shallow sliver of moving water. Diego stopped to peer through the dark night to see if he could discover a place to move through the trees and vegetation on the other side of the river. After a minute of looking up and down the river for a place to cross, he realized that two of the mustangs had already crossed the drying riverbed and were entering onto a path through the trees on the other bank.

"At least someone knows where we are going," the elderly man said to his horse. He then clicked his tongue and directed Oscuro across the river and followed the two mustangs. The other horses seemed to accept the black stallion's decision and followed. The two horses that had initiated the crossing cantered on into the New Mexico night heading west without hesitation. Diego determined that they knew where they were going, so he would just follow, hoping that the rest of the horses did likewise. They did.

Oscuro and Diego followed the two mustangs without hesitation, trusting that the two untamed equines would lead them safely through the dark desert. The lead mustang kept a quick and constant pace. It was an easy trot allowing each of the horses to stay with the herd. The night grew darker, and the stars shined brighter as they moved steadily west. Diego was surprised when he felt Oscuro slow and then stop, awakening him from a short slumber. It took a minute or so before Diego realized that they were at a watering hole. He looked around, trying to see any signs of the Comanche. He saw nothing to reinforce the feeling that they were trailing him, but he sensed that as soon as the sky lightened, he would need to quicken the pace, driving the small herd further into the west. He didn't realize that the two mustangs had been moving west-northwest, avoiding the rougher terrain near the mountains of central New Mexico.

After the horses had gotten their fill of water and had a reasonable rest, Diego climbed into his saddle and started to ride west. The herd immediately started to follow. Within a short distance, the same two mustangs trotted to the front of the group, retaking the lead. Diego laughed to himself when he realized that he wasn't leading the herd to freedom; the two elder mustangs were leading him to safety. He shook his head as he smiled and clicked his tongue, telling Oscuro to just follow the lead horses.

Dawn quietly snuck up on Diego. He hadn't noticed that the sky had begun to lighten until Oscuro whinnied and tossed his head. Don Diego stretched up in his saddle and looked around, first turning to his right and then turning as far to his left as he could. It was then that he saw the sun light gleaming off the top of a high mountain to his southeast. He hadn't noticed the high peak during the night, having concentrated on the two mustangs in front of him while carefully listening for the sound of any approaching riders. Although this land was new and strange to him, he felt an unexpected sense of comfort.

Everywhere he turned was a previously unseen vista, but the brown earth, the distant mountains, and the morning colors seemed warm and inviting. He felt a sense of coming home, of arriving at a place that he didn't know but knew him. He thought that he had arrived at a place that had been waiting for him.

Diego saw a small rise to the north and encouraged Oscuro to quickly run there and climb to the top of the higher ground. He looked to the east seeking any sign of the Comanche. To his satisfaction, he saw rising dust in the dim light, indicating that riders were in close pursuit. As he sat quietly atop his black stallion on that small hill, sunrays broke over mountains to the east and lit the precipice with morning brightness. Diego responded by yanking back on the reins and leaning back in his saddle, causing Oscuro to raise his two front legs and churn them slowly as he gathered his balance on his hind legs. The Comanche saw their quarry but were filled with dread as they saw the black-clad raider on his black beast standing tall and calling them to follow. They did so with dread, assured that something tragic awaited them.

8.

CHAPTER

The Chase Continues

The Comanche were relentless in their pursuit of the herd of horses and the man that took them. Diego rode down from the short hill and quickly rode to the front of the freed horses. Once Oscuro got to the lead, the weary rider indicated for the stallion to quicken the pace. The horses and man rode west, hoping that the Comanche would follow but not overtake them. Diego thought that it would be helpful if he could ride one of the other horses to relieve Oscuro of his weight. He scolded himself for not thinking about that at the waterhole when the horses were settled and busy drinking water.

That day was a blur to Diego. He had already gone over thirty hours without sleep, and he knew that the horses needed to rest. The herd continued a westerly course, and Diego became aware that Oscuro was tiring quickly. He saw a copse of juniper trees and small brush and decided to stop and dismount there. There was a small pond of water which the horses immediately surrounded. Diego removed the saddle from Oscuro and watched as his beautiful horse walked to the pond to share in the bounty of the water. Diego placed the saddle under the shade of three Junipers and settled to the ground, resting his head on the saddle. He thought a short rest would be prudent.

Diego was jogged from a deep, dreamless sleep by the whinny of the horses. It took a few seconds to remember where he was and the peril that he was in. He quickly saddled Oscuro. As soon as he mounted, the two elder mustangs started jogging into the west. Diego and the herd quickly followed.

After a short distance, Diego's head cleared, and he tried to determine if there was immediate danger from the Comanche. He noted that the sun was already well past its apex in the clear blue sky. He couldn't believe that he had slept so long. His thoughts returned to the wagon train and Gabriella, and he wondered if they had been able to run off the remaining Comanche. He prayed silently that they were safely on their way.

They continued their pace while Diego concentrated intently on any sighting or sound of the pursuers. They rode on into the late afternoon. Diego had no idea how far they had traveled or how far behind them were the Comanche raiders. He believed that he had to continue to move, to keep trotting into the unknown. They slowly made their way through shallow barrancas on well-worn paths created by the ancient ones and used by the wild animals of this high desert. When they could, they quickened their pace continuing onward into the west.

Diego saw a reddish-brown mound of stone in the distance and headed directly toward it. When they got there, he stopped Oscuro, stared at the high stone wonder, and decided that they would stop here. He had no idea at the distance they had traveled west, but he assumed that he was deep within Navajo territory. Diego dismounted, and after scrambling to the top of the outcropping and satisfying himself that the Comanche were not near, he removed the saddle from his equine friend. He brushed the stallion and then rubbed him with the saddle blanket. Diego allowed the horse to remain unsaddled while he ate some oats from Diego's hat. When Oscuro finished his meal, Diego saddled him but kept the cinch a little loose for the horse's comfort. If the Comanche approached, Diego wanted to be ready to move out quickly.

Diego climbed toward the top of the natural structure and found a small sandstone platform on which to sit. Although it blocked his view to the west and slightly blocked his view to the north, it provided a wide view to the east and south. He felt that he would be less obvious to any approaching riders than if he were on the summit. He sat and kept his eyes focused on the eastern horizon. He knew that twilight was not long off, followed by a profound darkness, which would clear when his eyes fully adjusted to the lack of any sunlight.

He thought he heard sounds in the distance. He thought he heard voices crying out. Then he heard the unmistakable sound of gunfire. As he squinted into the east, he thought he saw large clouds rising from beyond the horizon. A few of the horses neighed, and they drew closer to one another; then, they quickly calmed and continued to gnaw on the sparse desert vegetation. Diego decided there was no immediate danger, so he let the horses rest.

He spent the night on his stone throne, frequently changing positions in response to his aching back and buttocks. A few times, he startled himself from a restless sleep and stared out into the blackness of the darkened landscape. The night proved quiet and unremarkable.

It was still dark when Diego maneuvered down from his perch to find Oscuro. The black stallion came to him immediately and greeted him with a nudge from his large head. The man spoke softly to his horse, asking him if he was ready for a long run. The horse grunted a whinny as if to assure his master that he was prepared for whatever Diego needed. Some of the other horses moved closer to Diego, curious about the relationship between the man and the stallion. Diego greeted the group in a gentle voice, trying his best to keep them calm, but sensed that they were ready to move on.

Dawn came upon them quickly. Before Diego knew it, sunlight was peeking over the eastern horizon. He tightened the cinch around Oscuro before he scurried back up to his perch to retrieve his hat and sword. He placed his hat on his head and grabbed his sword. He quickly looked around the flat surface to make sure that he hadn't forgotten something. As he did, he noticed some movement on the horizon. He tried to focus on an object and thought it was a single horse and rider. He almost stumbled as he urgently went down the hillside.

He strapped on his rapier and mounted into his saddle. He knew that the rider had spotted him. There was no need to try to hide, so he tugged his reins and directed Oscuro toward the solo rider, turning his head from side to side to assure himself that there was no danger from either flank. He rode out about fifty yards toward the rider and halted his horse. They stood motionless as the rider continued to approach them.

When the rider was a couple of hundred yards from them, Diego pulled back on his reins and had Oscuro stand on his back legs. He then raised his hat and waved it over his head. It was his way of telling the approaching figure that they were healthy and strong and had no fear of him.

The rider continued his steady movement toward Diego. He stopped about fifty yards from him and raised his right hand in greeting. Diego responded by doing the same. The rider was a native, but did not look like the Comanche that

Diego had seen. He had colorful markings on his face and arms, and his horse also had markings.

The Indian spoke loudly in a tongue that Diego did not know. He often gestured with his arms and hands, indicating the surrounding land and then motioning toward the sky. He then pointed directly at Diego, placed his right hand on his left shoulder, and slid it to his heart. He then expelled a chant as he looked up into the sky. Finally, he raised his horse onto its back legs and held a spear above his head. As soon as the horse's feet hit the ground, the rider turned and began to trot back into the morning sun.

Diego sat quietly on Oscuro and watched as the remarkable Indian rode away. He stayed in that position until the rider had become nothing more than a blur on the horizon. When he got back to the herd of horses, the two mature mustangs whinnied and began to trot to the north. Some of the herd quickly followed, and some began to move further west. Just three horses waited for Oscuro and Diego.

Diego patted his friend on his long neck and said, "It's time for everyone to go their own way." It was then that Diego realized that he was missing his black mask. He sighed and looked up to the perch. He didn't want to climb back up there but believed that he must. He laughed at himself as he started his ascent. Fortunately, he now knew where the best footholds were. From the porch, he saw the black cloth mask laying eight or nine feet to the left of his perch and five feet below. After studying the position of the mask, he thought it would be best to first retreat a meter down before moving to the left. As he started to move to the left, he could see that there were few, if any, places to leverage his hands or feet. He moved cautiously as he approached the mask. He was pleased to find that he had reached a place close enough to grab the cloth if he stretched his left hand as far as he could. He made sure that his toes were firmly set in the stone, and his right hand was grabbing a firm hold.

Diego took a deep breath, moved his weight to his left foot, and reached out his left hand as far as he could. He was able to clutch the mask. He brought the cloth to his body and stuck it in his mouth to free the hand. As he raised his right hand to find a home to grasp, he could not locate the spot that he had previously held. He raised his head slightly to search for a hold. It was then that his left foot slipped. His right hand held tight in place, but for a few seconds, it supported his full weight. His body twisted and began to turn. He was able to find a foothold for his right foot, which prevented a fall down the rocky structure.

His left leg swung completely around until the back of the leg slammed into the wall. Diego immediately returned the swinging leg to his left side and found a spot that would support some weight. Although the fall would unlikely have killed him, the thought of serious abrasions or a broken bone worried Diego. He steadied himself and slowly started moving to his right. It was with great relief when he returned to a spot where he had climbed before.

He drew a deep breath in relief and congratulated himself on the successful rescue of his mask. The momentary lack of concentration was quickly punished as he began to slide down the steep surface of the stone edifice. His chest hit the stone wall, sending his body into a rapid twist, which resulted in his back hitting the same surface. He tried to find a hold to stop his downward slide with his heels and hands. To his amazement, his boots found two small platforms simultaneously, allowing his hands to grasp secure rock.

Diego stayed calm and quiet for almost a minute, attempting to determine his next move. He was aware that his black hat had fallen from his head, but this time he decided not to worry about a missing part of his clothing. He slowly rolled his head to the right, carefully keeping the back of his head in contact with the stone. The slide had caused him to be thrown a little to the left of his climbing route. He was unsure of how next to move, so he lowered his head slightly and studied the stone beneath and to the right of him. He decided that his only hope of avoiding another painful fall was to keep his weight on his right hand and heel and slowly move his left side around his right side.

Just as he was beginning to move his left leg, he heard the unmistakable sound of a rattler's tail, followed by a sharp pain on the back of his right thigh above the knee. The plummet down to the desert floor was sudden and painful. Diego landed hard on the ground after bouncing down the slope. He cautiously remained still before trying to move one body part at a time. His body was screaming with pain in various places, but he was aware that he did not hit his head in the fall. He slowly moved his arms, then his hands, then his legs. The relief that his limbs would move was quickly erased by the realization that he had a much bigger problem.

Diego slowly sat up and began to feel the back of his upper right thigh. He touched the bite wound and felt great pain. The bite was slightly below his buttock, making it impossible to see. His knife was still firmly held in its sheath on his hip. He anxiously cut the cloth away from the wound, knowing that he had to make a deep incision directly on the wound if he were to have any chance of survival.

Oscuro walked up to his master, who sat on the ground holding his knife in his right hand. He whinnied and nudged Diego's head as if asking if Diego was all right.

"Move back, *mi querido amigo*. I have to do this now while my hand is still steady." Without any further delay, Diego sliced a deep cut across the bite wound. He cried out in pain but immediately felt the wound again and then sliced across a second time, trying to cut across the previous slice. He shook with pain but held on tightly to his knife. Fortunately, he had a clean cloth in his pocket, which he tied over the wound as best he could. He then sliced a length of leather from the reins that he had removed from Oscuro, wrapped it around his right leg above the wound, and fastened it as tight as he could.

He knew that the more he moved the quicker the venom would spread, but he had to remove the saddle from Oscuro. Diego slowly stood up and used the stallion for support. His body ached in many spots, but the pain in his right leg was excruciating. He reached under his horse and loosened the cinch slowly. He then pulled the saddle from the horse's back, allowing it to fall to the ground. Oscuro turned and lowered his head in response to his master's gentle tug on the reins and allowed Diego to remove his bridle and the reins.

"Go, Oscurito. Find some fine mares and make handsome babies." Diego pulled the saddle to the rock formation, making sure that the front of the saddle faced away from the stone. He then sat on the saddle and leaned his back on a smooth stone, making sure that his wound was lower than his heart. The black stallion came forward and looked at the saddle and the rock, curious as to his master's actions.

"I told you to go. One of us must survive. Go find the herd and become a legend." The horse turned and walked about twenty meters away. Then he stopped and stood patiently, ignoring the commands of his master.

The venom began to affect the victim quicker than he thought it would. The first symptom was a chill that ran throughout his body. He grabbed the horse blanket, which he had dragged with the saddle, and held it over his chest and arms. Don Diego Vega sat staring at his horse and the horizon beyond. He felt a prickling around the top of his head, and he had trouble keeping his eyes focused. The blackness overcame him, and he lost consciousness.

The music in his dream sounded calming and sweet. The haunting tune from an unseen flute seemed to lift him up and relieve the burning in his right leg. He heard a gruff pleasant voice in a strange language. In the poison incited dream, an old man leaned over Diego, looking deeply at his face with such intensity that he seemed to see into the dying man's mind. The face had the red-brown color and weather-beaten look of the stone mound from which he had recently fallen. The stone man spoke in a language that he didn't recognize. Diego recognized that the ancient words were not meant for his ears but for his soul. Then Diego heard a horse's whinny, which made him think that Oscuro had disobeyed him. Soon Diego began to float, landing gently on a soft surface, and then began to sail on his back, looking at a bright blue sky. Finally, the dream faded into total darkness, with Diego feeling peaceful and free.

9.

CHAPTER

Klah Returns

Diego heard the music again, and felt a coolness come to his leg before returning to the addictive darkness. The next time he heard the extraordinary music, the stone man was above him, talking in that mystifying language, which soothed his being. He closed his eyes, trying to concentrate on the uncommon words, but quickly slipped into unconsciousness.

He was awakened by soft voices speaking yet another unknown language that did not speak to him in any manner, worldly or otherwise. He saw three male natives bent over him. They were obviously talking about him. Diego raised his right arm slightly to make them aware that he was conscious. One of the natives cautiously raised Diego's right leg and inspected it. He looked up at his two companions and spoke excitedly. They reacted with amazement and moved closer to look at the wounded leg.

Diego felt his head being lowered, causing him to be lying flat. Then he felt himself being lifted on what he assumed was a litter and carried into an unfamiliar setting. It was not a pueblo. The setting was much different than he had seen elsewhere in this amazing land. He felt comfortable for the first time since he fell as he was laid in front of the opening of a large tipi. The cone-shaped tent was covered by animal hides supported on wooden poles. He was lifted from his litter and carried into the warm tipi and placed on a bed, the softness of which surprised him.

Who had brought Diego to this band of natives was a mystery to him and, to his surprise, unknown to his hosts. Two days after arriving, Diego was lifted into a sitting position and fed a little solid food. As soon as he ate his small meal, he laid back down and fell asleep. The following day he spoke for the first time. He asked: where was he, what happened to the stone man, had they seen Oscuro? An old woman just stared at him silently, not knowing the meaning of his words. Later two males came to his bedside and to his relief, spoke to him in Spanish.

His questions were answered. They were Muache, a branch of the Utes. This small band were at this location to tend to their fields and would shortly return to their summer homes in the mountains to the north. The two Utes spoke of a nearby river, and Diego wondered if that could be the legendary *Rio de las Animus*, the River of Souls. It was then that he realized how far north and west he had traveled since leaving the wagon train on the Camino Real. He became anxious to see the surrounding country to see if it was as lush as described in the reports of the first Spanish explorers of the area.

One of the men asked Diego how he got on the travois and came to their location. Diego shared the details of his run from the Cherokee to his present predicament. He asked them what happened to the stone man that cared for him after his injury. They told him that there was no sign of anyone with him. They found him lying on a travois, being pulled by a black devil horse. No other person was with him. They asked him to give more detail about this man of stone. It was then he thought to reveal the strange sound of a flute and the man's soothing undecipherable words.

The second Indian explained in broken Spanish that they believed that Diego was rescued by an ancient spirit. The flute player is known to many tribes and has many faces. "Some know him as a trickster that brings chaos, others as the bearer of death, some as the guardian of unborn children, and to some, he is hope. He has many faces, but when in his human form, he has a weathered face and speaks the language of the Ancient Ones, which is no longer spoken. His face speaks of the many centuries of walking in the sun and wind. To reveal himself in human form is a great honor.

Diego sat quietly, trying to understand. He decided that such things were beyond him and asked about Oscuro.

The two Utes laughed. One asked, "Do you ride that monster?"

"Yes, of course."

"We have tried to catch him, but he charges us and then runs away like the wind. He stays near the camp. Only leaving to eat and drink. He returns and announces his presence by loud sounds and stamping feet. One of the children took a root to him, approaching him with caution. The devil-horse sat calmly eating from the child's hand. If anyone else approached, he would quickly back away."

"Take me out to him, so he can see that I am not dead." Diego nodded, "He needs to know if he should wait for me or leave to run with the wild ones."

Diego was assisted out of the tipi and then allowed to walk on his own to the perimeter of the small camp. The two men walked next to him in case he needed their help. They helped him sit on the ground and stepped back. Oscuro trotted near Diego, stopping many feet away and looking for any signs of danger. Satisfied, he whinnied and walked to his master, lowering his head, so Diego could scratch behind his ears.

"It is good to see you, my friend. I heard that you have been looking for me. I am sorry to have been away and to have caused you such concern." Diego asked the two Utes to help him to his feet. He stood supported by the men and patted Oscuro on his long neck. "We will ride again soon," he said softly and laid his head on the horse. The two stood quietly for many minutes.

Diego raised his head from the horse and nodded to his two new friends, "Take me back, please." The men supported him and turned to go back to the tipi. "Come along," Diego told the stallion, who then followed them into the camp.

Diego was awakened from his nap by one of the women who made the universal sign for eating to him. He nodded and sat up on his own. As he began to eat the stew with his hands, he heard the unmistakable whinny of his black stallion from outside the tipi. When he was done eating, the young woman helped him to get outside. He found Oscuro calmly standing near the tipi. Three young children walked around him in awe, staring at his high flanks and rubbing his deep-black hair. The children moved away quickly when they saw the stranger approach the horse.

"I see that you have made friends with the little ones, no?" he asked the horse. Oscuro nodded his large head. One of the men that he had met earlier in the day approached, greeting Diego in Spanish. Diego responded courteously and then asked, "Where are your horses?"

The man explained that they had only four horses and pointed in the direction of their locale. "Can my horse stay with them? I am sure his presence in the middle of your camp is not of your choosing." The tall Ute agreed and inquired if Diego was strong enough to walk on his own before leading him and the devil-horse to the small herd of ponies. Oscuro stood calmly while Diego placed a rope around his head and tied him with the other horses. As a reward, the Ute fed and watered Oscuro.

A few days later, Tonah-ah-ee, the taller of the two Spanish-speaking men, came to Diego to advise him that they would be returning to the mountains in three days and that he would need to be able to ride. If not, he would be pulled in a travois. To his relief, the Ute revealed that they found his saddle, blanket, and bridle with him when he arrived. Diego announced that at some point, he needed to get to Santa Fe.

"I have heard of this place," said Tonah-ah-ee. "I know of no Muache that have been there, but some of the other Utes have spoken of this place. The Spanish have been there for many years." The Indian pointed to himself and spoke of the things he heard about Santa Fe. "The Navajo and some Ute have had many battles with the Spanish there. They steal horses and children from one another. The Spanish live too close together and smell of rotten meat and onions. You should avoid that place."

"Are you friends of the Navajo?" asked Diego.

"We both claim this land as ours but have learned to share it. We spend the winter in a few canyons protected from the harshest winds and snow. They spend the winters in their winter places. So, neither of us roam the land during the winter. In the spring, we go back to our mountains."

"But, what of your fields? The Navajo do not steal your crops?"

"We all must live, *senor*. Like the Navajo, we depend on the harvest to feed us during the cold winter months. We quarrel every now and then, as young men will do silly things, but we have learned to live next to one another."

Diego continued to ask about the co-existence, "I know little about the Ute, but I do know that the Navajo raid the Spanish and other tribes for horses and children."

"That is true, but we also raid the Navajo. We all wish for more ponies and need fresh bloodlines to exist. It has been this way since the sun first shined," explained Tonah-ah-ee.

On the occasion when Diego learned the names of the two Spanish-speaking Utes, he tried to pronounce their names properly without much success. After many attempts to pronounce the two names, Tonah-ah-ee and Zai-koo-ko, the two men shrugged as if to say, "Close enough."

Diego was pleased that he seemed to quickly learn and accept their foreign ways. He tried to learn some of their words and closely observed how they interacted with one another. He wished he could understand their culture and group structure but had little success. As he began to walk around the camp on his own, all that he met greeted him kindly and treated him with respect. Even Oscuro was warmly welcomed. He was well fed and allowed to move with the other horses. It was evident that he had been brushed more than once.

On the day when he learned of their pending departure, Diego allowed children to be placed on Oscuro's back and then walked them through the camp. Each child held onto the horse's mane and smiled broadly at their families as they rode atop the big horse.

Afterward, Diego asked for his saddle. He refused any assistance to saddle the stallion and pulled himself up into the saddle. He then turned Oscuro and slowly trotted away from the camp. His stiff back and limbs complained with each gentle bounce. Eventually, he no longer felt any discomfort and quickened his pace. He followed a narrow trail west a short distance until he came to the river. Diego smiled broadly as he heard the moving water and saw the green growth along its banks. He was startled by the change in the appearance of the land; the endless tan and brown was replaced by green and other colors. It was not lush as he had known all his life, but in comparison to the desert, it was Eden.

He rode back to the camp and carefully dismounted. He almost fell from the weakness in his legs when he first stood on the ground, but he managed to balance himself with the help of his horse. One of the men came to remove the saddle for him, but Diego tactfully stopped the Ute, explaining as best as he could that he had to do it himself. Diego's arms strained and shook as he pulled the saddle from the horse and set it on the ground. The Ute ignored him, picked up the saddle, and carried it to Diego's tipi. The women that shared the large tent with Diego told the man where to place it and went to find their charge. They scolded the Spaniard as they walked him to the tipi. One of the women stayed to brush Oscuro after his short adventure. The horse whinnied in appreciation.

The next morning Zai-koo-ko entered the tipi carrying Diego's black hat, cape, and mask. "We have been holding these until you could ride again." He handed the items to the Spaniard. "It is not our way to ask personal questions, but I am curious. Why do you have a mask?"

"I do not mind your question. You are my friends." Diego sighed, "As a much younger man, I got angry at how the authorities and the wealthy took advantage of those that had so little. The poor and those without any power were abused by the mighty. I tried to help as much as one man could." Diego held up the black cloth mask, "I had to hide my face from the authorities and the evil men. My actions would have placed my family in grave danger. Although I disagreed with my father on many things, I loved him as a son should. I used this mask to protect him and others from punishment for things that I had done.

"Unfortunately, my efforts were of little consequence. Nothing of substance was changed. If one corrupt man was removed, he was replaced by one that was even more ruthless and cruel. Eventually, I found a woman that I cherished, and I stopped riding the countryside trying to right that which was wrong."

"Did you have a good life with this woman that you loved?"

"Yes, but for only a short time. She died two years later in childbirth along with our only child." Diego looked up at Zai-koo-ko, "Then, for a long time, I lived the life of a shallow and selfish man. I wasted many years thinking only of myself and forgot that others had lost more than I." He smiled at the patient Indian, "The ancient flute player would have found little to like in that man. With the help of many that loved me, I tried to become a warrior for the unfortunate but was overwhelmed by the greed and hate of my own people. So, I came to this land looking for something better. Looking for a way to make a difference, looking to put my soul at peace."

"Do you think you will find it in this land?"

"No."

Later that morning, three riders came to the camp from the east. Tohna-ah-ee explained to Diego that the men were Navajo and wished to speak with him.

Tonah-ah-ee acted as interpreter for the council. The women brought food and water for the men to share and then sat behind the Utes and Diego. The spokesman for the Navajo nodded his approval of the respect shown to Diego. He then spoke for many minutes and waited patiently for his words to be interpreted for Diego. The tall Ute told Diego that the spokesman's name was Klah and that, as is the custom of the Navajo, he identified his mother's clan and then his father's clan.

The Ute gave his name, his mother's family name. Diego then said, "I am Diego of the house of Vega and Tantanto from Seville through California. Are you the man that I saw by the stone mound?"

Tonah-ah-ee translated the family information to the Navajo but did not ask Diego's question. He explained to Diego, "He has come to us and asked to speak. It would be impolite to ask him a question before he explained his reason for coming to speak to you." He glanced at the three Navajo and then back at Diego, "It is their way."

Klah waited until the Muache had finished speaking to Diego. "I came to take you to Narbona, who has asked that you come to him. He is with our band waiting to see if the Comanche return seeking revenge for the loss of the raiding party that had been following you." Klah watched Diego until he was sure that he understood his words. "We watched you as you and your tall horse lead the stolen ponies away from the Comanche. When you stopped at the Red-Rock-That-Stands, we set a trap for them." The Indian snarled, "They were foolish and did not look for us. We charged from the south, causing them to seek protection to the north, only to find a larger group waiting for them. The Comanche died bravely."

Diego nodded, "I saw the dust rising into the sky and heard the cries of men in battle."

The Navajo sat quietly, not surprised at the white man's rudeness. He wondered why these white men could not control their tongues while others were speaking. "We were not sure what kind of creature we saw. He looked like a man dressed in black, riding a large black horse, but he could be the Coyote tricking the Comanche to their deaths. It was for that reason I followed you to the Red-

Rock-That-Stands. I wanted to see if you were a man or an ancient spirit. I was startled as you seemed to come out of the red stone to show yourself, but when I saw you climb down the face of the stone and mount your horse, I thought you were just a man.

"You rode forward calmly, showing that you were not frightened and meant me no harm. When I got close and saw your unmasked face, I was satisfied that you were of this world. Then, I rose my horse in salute to your bravery and cunning. You responded with a salute.

"When I got back to Narbona and reported my findings," Klah indicated his companions, "he asked these two young men to return to the Red-Rock-That-Stands to bring you to him. They returned two days later and said that you were not there, and there were no signs of how you left and no signs of you ever being there.

"Narbona then ordered me to go with them to try to find you." Klah waved his left arm in a circle, "We rode in all directions and found no signs of you or your black stallion. We came to this camp when I remembered that these mountain dwellers would come to tend their fields. This is how I found you." Klah momentarily sat silently and then looked at Tonah-ah-ee.

The Ute spoke directly to the Navajo for a while. Diego assumed he was explaining how they had found him outside of their camp, lying on a travois. Tonah-ah-ee spoke for a long time, causing Diego to wonder what he was saying to the Navajo.

Both Indians turned toward Diego, "Why did one man need so many horses?" asked the Navajo.

"I did not need horses. I needed the Comanche to follow me," replied Diego.

"Why did you come into the Dinatah?"

"I do not know where your land starts and stops. I just wanted them to follow me west, away from our wagons on the Camino Real, so my people could reach safety."

"The Comanche would have tortured you for as long as they could before they let you die. You made them chase horses that they had already stolen. Why would you just not give them back the horses?"

"We had rescued some hostages that they kidnapped from Santa Fe, killing two warriors in the process. If they lost the horses, they would have nothing from their raids."

Klah thought about this and then asked, "How do you know the ways of the Comanche?"

Diego laughed, "I knew nothing of the Comanche, but I know the heart of greedy men. A companion had previous experience with the Comanche, and he seemed to know a lot about them."

"How is this companion called?" asked Klah.

"He is a young man named Kit Carson," answered Diego.

It was Klah's turn to laugh, "I have met this young man. He knows many tongues."

"He is a courageous man of good character," stated Diego.

Klah nodded but added, "He is still in his youth, and his heart is not finished. His true character is not known to him yet."

Diego nodded quietly in reply.

"Tell me of the man that brought you to the Muache."

Diego slowly told all that he could remember of the old man and his stone face.

The next morning Diego and Oscuro left the camp with the three Navajo. Diego was sad to leave his two friends and the pleasant band of Muache. He clumsily attempted to shake hands with Tonah-ah-ee, who had no experience with this European custom. The Ute said words in his own language and tossed leaves and dust in the four directions. He finished by dropping some of the mix on Diego.

10.

CHAPTER

Narbona

The four men rode into Narbona's camp three days later. They were fed and allowed to rest before Diego was brought to the tall, muscular leader. Diego had been surprised to learn that Klah was fluent in Spanish. The Navajo revealing his skill shortly after leaving the Muache. Although this initially disturbed Diego, he was pleased to have someone to communicate with on the trip.

Diego waited as Narbona greeted him in the traditional manner. Diego responded in kind and then waited for Klah to interpret. The leader of this large band of Navajo explained that he wanted to see the black shadow that rode with ponies across the Dinetah, the man in black that the Comanche could not catch, the man that lured their enemy to their death.

The rest of the conversation was exactly as Diego's initial discussion with Klah. Narbona then invited Diego to stay with his people for as long as he desired but suggested that he should remain with them for at least two cycles of the moon.

The first two nights in the Navajo camp, Diego slept in the home of Klah, sharing the tipi with his wife and two children. Tiponi had been taken from the Hopi as a young maiden and was quickly claimed by Klah. She had been his wife for six years and was pregnant with their third child. Diego quickly made friends of their two children, especially with the five-year-old son, Manuelito. As he had done with the Muache children, Diego put Manuelito on Oscuro's back and walked him around the camp. The little boy beamed with pride as he sat high on the stallion.

On the third day, Diego was told that he would sleep and eat in the tent of a young widow. He strongly objected, but Klah explained that this woman's husband had died in a fall from his horse. The horse had stumbled while in full gallop, falling to the ground and tossing its rider over its head. The young man landed on his head, striking a rock, and breaking his neck. The widow was left without any family. Her husband had no brother to take his place, and her mother had died years before. She has been by herself for many months and has become the target of cruel words and taunts from the other women. If Diego stayed with her, it would give her much prestige, as he is a respected guest of Narbona and a friend of Klah.

Shideezhil was a pleasant, small woman who was eager to welcome this strange man into her tipi. She fussed over her lodger, cooking good meals, cleaning his clothing, and providing a comfortable place to sleep and live. Diego was surprised at how tiny she was. She looked to weigh less than fifty kilos and stood less than one and a half meters. The young woman may have had an attractive face at one time, but she had scarred herself in mourning her husband. It was a custom for young Navajo widows to scar their arms, but Shideezhil had gone further and cut both cheeks with two long lines.

Narbona often asked Diego to join him, so they could discuss their views of the world. The tall chief wanted to learn all he could of the Spanish and taught his guest much about the Navajo. Both men were baffled by the peculiar customs of the other's culture. Diego told of his disgust with the greed and cruelty of his own people. He explained he left Mexico because he could no longer live amongst all the avarice and hate.

"Why did you not stay and try to get your people on the correct path?" asked the Chief.

Flustered by the accusatory nature of the question, Diego had to calm himself before answering, not wanting to offend his host with an emotional response. "As a young man, I wore my black mask and rode the great grandfather of Oscuro. I tried to right the wrongs done to the unfortunate ones. I had some success, but I made no significant change in the actions of the powerful and the wrongs committed against the poor. As an older man, I went to the large council of leaders and was constantly ignored. I was taunted by those who had the authority of power, shunned by those that feared the powerful, and finally threatened with my life. I left beaten and humbled."

"I know men such as these," responded Narbona. "They have dark hearts and have forgotten the stories of origin. They have been in the darkness for so long that they cannot find Hozho. They will never find peace and balance in their lives. It is dangerous to have these men as leaders."

To Narbona's surprise, Diego spoke of other people that were even worse than the Spanish. He had known about the other white people far to the east, but he had never heard their names. His guest spoke of the English, the Dutch, the Germans, and others that lusted for wealth and land. Others that have abused and eliminated natives wherever they have gone. Narbona decided to call the people that Diego spoke of "The Others from Elsewhere". He understood that one day they would come to the Dinetah, and the Dine must be ready to fight for their home.

One day Klah took Diego to hunt rabbits and birds. The two men arranged snares in a place known for rabbits and by some nests on two mesas in hopes of snaring a few large birds. They spent the night at the base of a mesa, choosing not to make a fire. The sounds of the dark night reminded Diego of the nights he spent by himself when he outran the pursuing Comanche. He remembered that the purpose of that excursion was to protect his beloved Gabriella and his friends. He felt a pang of longing to see her and hold her close. He fell asleep, wondering if he would ever see her again.

Shideezhil shrieked in excitement when Diego came to her tipi proudly holding two rabbits. She called out to the other women exclaiming her guest's prowess as a hunter and provider. The widow quickly skinned and gutted the two rabbits, carefully cleaning them with water to remove blood and bits of fur and setting the gizzards aside. Diego did not watch her prepare the meal but went to see Manuelito, to present him with a unique stone that he had found the day before. When Shideezhil served him dinner, he was dumbfounded that she prepared the meat in a stew with roots and chilis rather than roasting it over a fire. However, he was pleased by the tenderness of the meat and the sweet tang of the sauce. She watched him with wide eyes and smiled when he obviously enjoyed his meal.

A few days later, the young widow, whose name meant Little Sister, presented him with a shirt and leggings made of soft leather. With her hands, she told him she had made these for him. He thanked her warmly, placed the clothing on his bed, and tried to explain to her that these were special. He would wait to wear them the next time Narbona called for him. It was clear that she didn't quite understand and was hurt that he did not wear them immediately. Later that afternoon, he brought Klah to her to explain his decision to wait until he went to the chief to wear his new clothes. She smiled when she heard the explanation.

Klah had Diego walk with him back to his tipi. "That widow has become attached to you and wishes for you to become her husband despite your many years. It is not uncommon in our culture and is accepted by all, especially when the young woman is a widow."

"My friend, she is a gifted young woman and is pleasant to be with, but I have a deep love for another. Someone that I have just begun to know and miss with all my heart. When it is the right time, I will leave you and go to Santa Fe to my Gabriella and my Spanish life."

"Many men have more than one wife. Some even share the same tipi. Why could you not have a Navajo wife and a Santa Fe wife?"

"When I get to Santa Fe, it will be hard for me to return to the Dine. I will begin my new life with a new bride. I may never return. That is not right for Shideezhil. She would be alone again. I would never do that to her. She is still young and needs a young man to give her children and a permanent love. I have a great attachment to her, but it is the love of a brother, not a lover."

"Then you must tell her of your Gabriella. She has already gained much from you living with her. When you leave, she will find many prospects. You should also tell Narbona of her and how pleasant and strong she is. When he welcomes her friendship, the young men will fly to her."

"Let's speak with her tomorrow," suggested Diego.

That evening as he prepared for bed, Little Sister came up to him and took the clothes that she had given him. She folded them neatly and placed them on a rug next to his bedding. She smiled at him and gave him a longing look. He knew that she needed tender affection and wanted him to invite her to his bed. He was embarrassed by the strong urge to accept her offer, but felt it would be a selfish act. He smiled as tenderly as he could and shook his head slightly. He then lay on his bed and turned away from her.

The next morning Klah came to visit early and found an anxious Diego waiting in front of the tipi. The Navajo almost laughed at his friend's obvious anxiety.

"Come in," Diego said quickly and led Klah into the tipi. They found the young woman sitting quietly, staring at the ground in front of her. Diego worried about her pain caused by the rejection by an old man. His heart felt her sorrow and pain.

With Klah interpreting, Diego told her of the loss of his first wife and child. He then explained his loneliness that followed and the eventual belief that he would never be able to love again. He smiled as he told of the rescue of Gabriella and their unexpected love. He told her that he would go to Gabriella as soon as Narbona and he agreed that it was time for him to leave. Finally, Diego addressed her as *asti*, the Navajo word for niece. She immediately understood Diego's strong bond to her as a brother's child and recognized that he would believe any romantic relationship would be taboo.

The next day Narbona called for Diego and Klah. Diego was very self-aware as he walked through the camp to join Narbona wearing the leather shirt and pants that Shideezhil had made for him.

She watched him with pride as he walked away after smiling at her.

They moved the large camp further west and south, finding a fresh spot to graze their sheep. Narbona continued to send small parties out to watch for signs of raiding intruders or foolish Mexican troops. When the Navajo Chief wanted to hide from an enemy, he was never found, seeming to be able to become invisible. When he knew that he had the advantage, he and his warriors would wait patiently for their prey to come to them.

 As the following weeks went by, Diego felt an ebbing of his energy. He was not expected or even allowed to do any chores. As a guest, he was exempt from the little chores that adult men performed, and Narbona would not allow him to join any of the scouting parties. The only thing he was permitted to do was ride Oscuro or hunt for small game if Klah or another trusted male was with him. When he returned from these outings, he was always exhausted. Shideezhil explained to him that the venom from the rattlesnake was still in him, and it was natural to tire easily.

The nights were beginning to get a little cooler as fall was approaching, causing Diego to seek

Narbona's permission to leave. The chief understood his guest's need to return to his people but asked that Diego wait until the next full moon, which was a little more than a week away. Narbona's reason for doing this was to assure that Klah and a few of his braves were available to escort Diego to the edge of Navajo land.

After a short ride one morning, He felt a sharp pain under his left shoulder blade as he removed the saddle from his black stallion. Klah heard his gasp of pain and asked his friend about it. Diego told him that he was having some back pain, which he was sure was from lack of sufficient physical activity. That afternoon Klah took Diego to the banks of a nearby shallow stream, where he had arranged a tent into a sweat lodge for the two of them. At first, Diego found the heat and steam irritating but said nothing to his friend. As he got used to the heat, he began to feel his muscles loosen and his heart slow. Then Klah placed some herbs and leaves on the steaming stones, causing a satisfying aroma to fill the sealed tent. Klah then started to chant softly. The words meant nothing to Diego, but he silently enjoyed the rhythmic sound of Klah's voice as his mind relaxed and wandered on its own.

When Klah announced that it was time to leave, Diego was disappointed. He could have stayed in that sweat lodge for hours longer. Klah had him sit on a stone near the creek and slowly poured water over his back and chest. Diego ignored the feel of the cold water, enjoying the subsequent tingle on his body. The two men wrapped themselves in blankets and walked back to the camp. Shideezhil was waiting for Diego and had him lay on the stomach on his bed. Then she rubbed a loose paste on his back with her warm hands. He fell into a deep sleep, wakening when Little Sister began to clean off his back. After the evening meal, he went to bed and slept through the night. He awoke the next morning feeling better than he had since the rattlesnake had bitten him.

11.

CHAPTER

Diego Departs

His departure from Narbona's camp was bittersweet. He hadn't realized how attached he had become to this group of Navajo. Narbona responded to Diego's words of thanks and respect with a broad smile and the hope that he would see his friend again. Then he gave Diego a Navajo name, Tse Chaha'oh, the meaning of which was Shadow from the Stone. Klah later explained to Diego that receiving your name from such an exalted leader was a great honor. He also explained that the reasons Narbona's gave the name in Klah's presence was that he considered Klah to be Diego's brother, and he needed Klah to explain the name to Tse Chaha'oh.

The farewell was difficult for both Diego and Shideezhil. She openly wept, and he held her close and fought back the tears as he addressed her. "I will never forget the kindness and love of my little niece. My spirit will always be with you, and I will remember you forever. I hope that you can accept a young man into your life with an open heart and have many children."

"I will look for you on your black stallion every day at dusk. My heart will ache until I see you again, Uncle." Those were her last words to Diego.

Manuelito stood quietly, holding the reins of Oscuro as Diego approached. The Spaniard said, "Goodbye, my young friend. I know you will follow in your father's footsteps and become a fine and noble man. I am certain that you will be a great leader of your people."

The young boy hugged him and handed him the reins.

Diego, Klah, and four braves rode out of the camp, looking forward without glancing back. Klah told Diego that if a leaving rider looked back, the people of the camp would see it as a sign of uncertainty and of lurking danger. Diego fought the urge to look back at these people whom he had learned to respect and care for, but heeded Klah's advice in acceptance of Navajo tradition.

As dusk neared, the six men ate a cold meal and began to settle in for the night. They picked the top of a small hill to make their camp. Klah pointed out the four sacred mountains of the Dine in the distance that marked the boundaries of the Dinetah. "Seeing these four mountains makes me feel at peace knowing that as long as I am within them, I am at home. You should know, Tse Chaha'oh, that these mountains are now part of your heart and being. They will forever be your home as they are mine."

They slept well that night, but Diego woke up with a sore left shoulder and arm. He must have slept on his left side, he told himself. When he saddled Oscuro, he felt discomfort under his left shoulder blade and gently rotated his shoulder and raised his arms over his head to stretch the aching muscle. That day they rode hard, taking only one rest to water the horses. That evening they stopped at a grassy area that looked familiar to Diego. It reminded Diego of the place where he and Oscuro had rested with the pack of wild horses.

Klah informed him that they would reach the end of Navajo lands by noon the next day. They built a fire and roasted some game that two braves had hunted earlier in the day. Diego ate little. The pain in his back and his weariness from the long ride made him crave sleep more than food. Despite this, he sat with his companions until Klah said that they should put out the campfire and rest.

Diego was not asked to help keep watch, but knew that the five other men would be careful and alert of what may approach them. He fell into a deep sleep, dreaming of Gabriella. She had a young child with her and ran into Diego's arms. Manolo and Safwan came to him, excited that he had finally returned to them. He slept on, and his dreams changed. He was returning to Narbona's camp and found Shideezhil with a child nursing at her breast and a proud Navajo brave at her side. They greeted him warmly and lovingly, offering him a place in their tipi. Narbona and Klah rode their horses to the tipi and called for their friend, Narbona telling Tse Chaha'oh that he is needed while handing him his black mask. As he was talking to the Navajo Chief, he heard Gabriella's voice calling to him, telling him that she missed him and would always love him. Then the dream slowly dimmed and turned to black. Diego took his last shallow breath with his head laying on Oscuro's saddle.

Klah cried in the morning when he found that life had left his friend. He wept, knowing that his friend's name would never be uttered again, as the Navajo avoided any mention of the dead for fear of their ghost coming to them. Klah convinced one of the braves to help him take the human remains of the man that once was to a hidden place. They would ride directly back to Narbona's camp and have a *hatali* performed, a cleansing for them to remove any ghost dust. Fortunately, the man that was his friend died outside, allowing his spirit to rise and float into the sky.

Two weeks after Diego's death, Shideezhil was on the edge of their camp at sunset. She was leaving scraps of food for the dogs that followed their camp. She thought of the stranger that became her uncle, and her heart filled with sorrow. It was then that she saw some movement out in the vast landscape. She stared where she thought she saw a dark figure. The figure moved closer, then seemed to grow taller. She gasped when she saw the dark figure waving his black hat over his head as his black stallion stood on its hind legs.

Ever since, there have been sightings of the man in black in the Dinetah. At times he is waving his hat in the air as his black stallion stands on its back legs or he and Oscuro are galloping across the desert floor. Often, he is sitting upon a rock formation…like a shadow from a stone.

AUTHOR BIOGRAPHY

After a thirty-year career in banking and three years of retirement, Phil decided to attempt to complete his lifelong dream of writing a novel. Starting with a blank page and only an idea of a plot, he completed Skating in the Moon Shadows sixteen months later. Subsequently he wrote a second Frank Triano novel, The Last Prayer. With the encouragement of his wife, his sons, and his friends, Phil continues to write daily. Shadow From the Stone is a significant change, as Phil ventures into the old west and the life of an established literary hero. This resident of Northeast Ohio has a fervor for writing, driven by his passion for the written word. As a child in Youngstown, Ohio he was introduced to books at an early age by his sisters and has been an avid reader ever since.

NOTES FROM THE AUTHOR

Thank you for your support in reading this short adventure. I originally envisioned this as a graphic novel but time did not allow for that, so I wrote the story with the hope that it will lead to other similar adventures. This is my first attempt at something other than a detective story and the process was very fulfilling.

As a man in his mid-seventies, I have wonderful memories of Don Diego Vega and his black clad alter ego. It's hard to believe that the character was created in 1918 and has appeared in movies and television ever since. It's a testament to Johnston McCulley's creative skills and storytelling.

Other stories by Phillip Suarez

Frank Triano Crime Novels:

<u>Skating in the Moon Shadows</u> (Triano Story 1)

<u>The Last Prayer</u>(Triano Story 2)

Shadow of a Crime (Triano Story 3) – Coming soon

Books available online at:

amazon.com

barnes&noble.com

Contact Phillip Suarez at:
suarezstories@gmail.com
phillipsuarez.com